NATASHA WING'S
The Night Before
Class Picture Day

Grosset & Dunlap
An Imprint of Penguin Random House

To all you photographers who make us look good—NW

To the one and only Shutter Speed Kid . . . with love—AW

GROSSET & DUNLAP
Penguin Young Readers Group
An Imprint of Penguin Random House LLC

Text copyright © 2016 by Natasha Wing. Illustrations copyright © 2016 by Penguin Random House LLC. All rights reserved.
Published by Grosset & Dunlap, an imprint of Penguin Random House LLC, 345 Hudson Street, New York, New York 10014.
GROSSET & DUNLAP is a trademark of Penguin Random House LLC. Manufactured in China.

Library of Congress Cataloging-in-Publication Data is available.

ISBN 978-0-448-48902-5   10 9 8 7 6 5 4 3 2 1

NATASHA WING'S

The Night Before

Class Picture Day

By Natasha Wing

Illustrated by Amy Wummer

Grosset & Dunlap
An Imprint of Penguin Random House

'Twas the night before picture day
and in homes everywhere,
all the parents were fretting
over unruly hair.

Children with straight locks
soon would have curls.

Boys' bangs were trimmed up,
    and so were the girls'.

Then they practiced in front
of their mirrors for a while,

until they perfected
a most flattering smile.

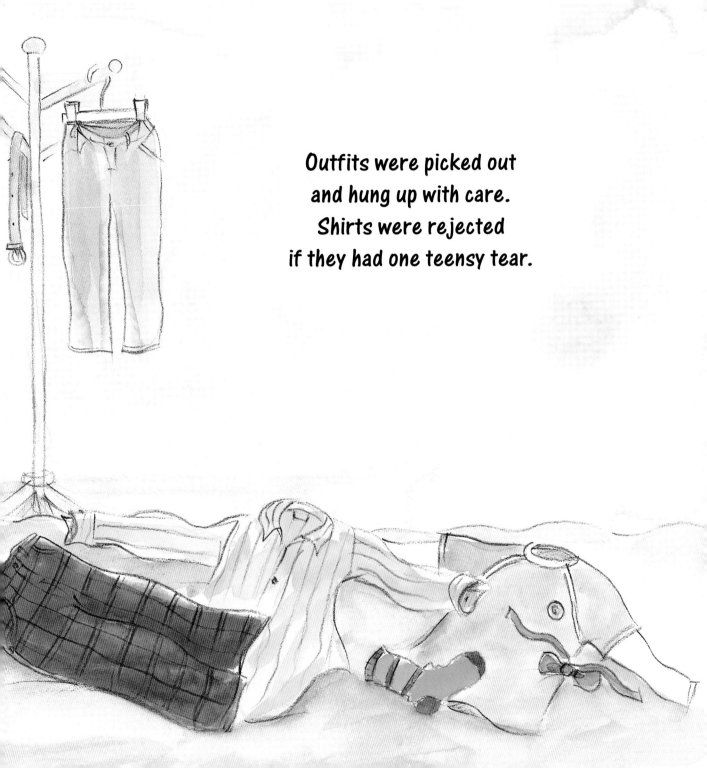

Outfits were picked out
and hung up with care.
Shirts were rejected
if they had one teensy tear.

The children then nestled
all snug in their beds,
while visions of cameras
flashed in their heads.

The next morning came warnings:
"When you play at recess,
I don't want you getting
any dirt on your dress."

"Remember to smile!" parents called,
still making a fuss.
"We will," kids chimed back
as they climbed on the bus.

Everyone stayed clean—
they truly did their best . . .

But then it was recess.
This would be the big test!

In a great game of dodgeball,
things got a touch out of hand.
Not everyone stayed tidy
as their parents had planned.

José lost a tooth,
and Rob tore his shirt.
Lizzy lost her bow,
and Kim stained her skirt.

But that didn't stop
the photographer that day.
With a "Look here and smile!"
she—*flash*—clicked away!

The children all left
with a souvenir comb.

A week later came pictures
of themselves to take home.

When what to their parents' eyes should appear
but a packet of photos of their little dear.

Their smiles—oh so smiley!
Their teeth—pearly white!

"Oh no! What's that?"
some moms said with fright.

There was jam on someone's glasses,
and blue paint on someone's nose.

Most eyes were wide open,
but a few were tightly closed.

Still, most families were happy—
their photos turned out okay.
For the others, thank goodness,
there's a do-over day!